THE
REPLACEMENT
CENTRE

FFLUR DAFYDD

The Replacement Centre
Published in Great Britain in 2022
by Graffeg Limited.

Written by Fflur Dafydd copyright © 2022.
Designed and produced by Graffeg Limited copyright
© 2022.

Graffeg Limited, 24 Stradey Park Business Centre,
Mwrwg Road, Llangennech, Llanelli,
Carmarthenshire, SA14 8YP, Wales, UK.
Tel: 01554 824000. www.graffeg.com.

Fflur Dafydd is hereby identified as the author
of this work in accordance with section 77 of the
Copyrights, Designs and Patents Act 1988.

A CIP Catalogue record for this book is available from
the British Library.

The publisher acknowledges the financial support of
the Books Council of Wales. www.gwales.com.

Printed and bound in Great Britain by Clays Ltd,
Elcograf S.p.A.

ISBN 9781802580846

1 2 3 4 5 6 7 8 9

THE REPLACEMENT CENTRE

FFLUR DAFYDD

GRAFFEG

Chapter 1

A week after Lloyd dies, I see an advert on TV about the Replacement Centre. It shows a woman kneeling by a grave and weeping into a tissue, her hair tied back into a bun. Seconds later, the same woman appears, hair flowing freely, walking hand in hand with a handsome man.

Throw away your tissues, the voice-over tells me. *Consider a replacement.*

'It's a brand-new scheme,' Mrs Evermoor next door tells me. She visits daily now, laden with food I have no desire to eat. Rather odd concoctions like upside down banana tarts, tuna lasagnes and miniature Christmas trees carved out of watermelons.

'They can find someone for you right away, who looks more or less exactly like the person you've just lost,' she says, lining the food up in front of me, like I'm going to be taking part in some kind of all-you-can-eat challenge.

'Melissa next door got lucky with hers. Truth

be told, I think she got a bit of an upgrade.'

I manage a mouthful of the sickly banana tart before promising to eat the rest of it later.

That evening I stand out in the front garden and watch over the fence as Melissa's husband puts the bins out. A big, burly man with broad shoulders and a good head of hair. He seems to know exactly which bin goes where, better than Lloyd ever could. It strikes me that I've never really noticed this man before, let alone realised he's a replacement for someone else. I struggle to remember what the first husband looked like. I don't remember him dying, even. Grief is like that, I suppose. It seems you never really take an interest until it happens to you. Then it's like being part of a club, one you haven't signed up for, but your membership is automatically renewed, whether you like it or not.

Still, I wonder how I missed it, the fact that Melissa's husband died, just like that, a few doors down, while Lloyd and I were getting on with our lives, bickering about whose turn it was to put the bins out. How could she have kept the whole thing so quiet? 'A drink problem, I suspect,' Mrs Evermoor says, 'no one ever knows what to say, do they? Poor Melissa.'

Poor Melissa seems to be getting on fine,

because I can see her now, in the window, smiling at her replacement husband as he walks back towards the house. She's got a little girl perched on her hip who raises her hand to wave at her dad. The little girl was only six months old when it happened, apparently, so they thought it best not to tell her. You can't really tell the difference from the photos, or so Mrs Evermoor says.

Melissa's husband suddenly looks up and catches me staring at him. He smiles kindly and says, 'Do you want me to sort yours too?'

I'm confused for a second, thinking he's offering me a new husband, until I realise he's referring to the bins.

'That would be very helpful,' I say and walk back indoors.

A replacement, I say to myself with disbelief, the word echoing in my mind. It reminds me of being a child again, weeping at the side of the road over my poor, dead, runover cat, only to have my father come home the next evening with a trembling six-week-old kitten and for the whole sorry business to be swept away in a ball of fluff.

Chapter 2

Three days later, I see the advert again. I start to get paranoid that they, the big, bad forces out there, know what has happened to me and that by searching up *best foods to fight cancer* and *how to tell chemo is working* and *symptoms for end stage of cancer* and *how long does it take someone to die* and then *eco-friendly coffins* that they know exactly what I've been through. I imagine a boardroom somewhere where a gang of millennials are huddled, saying things like: *ok, we imagine our ideal consumer to be someone mid-thirties, freshly bereaved, slightly disorientated, who is looking to fill the gaping hole at the centre of her universe. How can we reach her? She's unlikely to be going back to work for a while.*

That much is true. I went in last week, but it was a disaster. I can't remember crawling underneath my desk, like Sonya from HR said I did, but I know they had to drag me out by my feet and leave me in the staff room with the blinds down for the whole after-noon, much to the annoyance of those whose packed lunches were in the fridge I was sobbing against.

I heard the head of department offering to take them all out to a restaurant. Nice that they got something out of it, because he isn't usually that generous.

Compassionate leave, I think Sonya from HR called it in the end. I think they all know I won't be back. Because how can you ever go back, when something like this happens? There is no going back, is there? To anything, really.

I mope around the house wearing Lloyd's pyjamas for the next couple of days. They're extra-large and make me feel as if I'm getting too small for my own life. I flick the TV on and off, on and off. I become obsessed with a show about a hotel, a precinct drama they call it, which is about nothing really, it's just a load of people in a hotel, talking, walking in and out of rooms. I've become so sucked into it that I think I'm in the hotel with them. I imagine I see Lloyd among the cast and that he's no longer dead, he's just a concierge in a crappy precinct drama, which would be better than being in a pot on my mantlepiece.

A few days later, a letter arrives for Lloyd. When I open it up a colourful postcard falls out.

On the front is a picture of a villa in some hot country, though it doesn't say on the postcard where it is. Whoever sent it obviously doesn't know he's dead, because its tone is cheery and bright: *HI LLOYD! All well here. Can't wait to see you again!* Signed simply 'R' with a kiss, the way people sign off when they think they've reached that level of intimacy with someone. It's like the fewer letters they use, the less of a distance there is between them and the other person.

I lie on my side and get sucked into the TV again. But I find it hard to concentrate. That postcard really bothers me. Lloyd never mentioned knowing anyone abroad. Although I push the thought to the back of my mind, I'm now worried that maybe the Lloyd I've put on a pedestal, the Lloyd I thought I'd never be able to replace, was already trying to replace me when he died.

Right at that moment, something catches my eye, forcing me into an upright position. A little notice on the right-hand corner of the screen that tells me that the next item on the magazine programme I'm watching is about the Replacement Centre.

A man comes on and starts talking about how he lost his wife, Rosalie, last year to anorexia. The man says that he could never have imagined anyone replacing Rosalie, but that when he saw Rose he knew that it was OK to start again.

Replacement Rose looks off as her new husband prattles on. No one explains anything about how it can be possible for a real, live, breathing woman like Rose to just suddenly appear and be transplanted in someone else's life. In two minutes the item is over and the presenter turns his attention to the next item about book clubs, leaving the husband and come-from-nowhere wife smiling uncertainly into the camera.

For the rest of the day I just lie there on the purple carpet looking at the clouds moving above me in the sky outside and try to roll away with them, to some nowhere place, like the place Rose came from.

I start to think that it wouldn't be so bad, for someone to emerge out of those clouds now, and fill this gap in my universe.

Like the mysterious 'R' on that postcard filled the gap in Lloyd's. A gap I never knew existed.

Chapter 3

I turn up on Melissa's doorstep unannounced, still dressed in Lloyd's pyjamas. I know, from the look on her face, what a fright I must look – I haven't washed in days, and my hair, which is unruly at the best of times, seems to have bunched up around my face in a kind of mushroom cloud. She leans forward, trying to locate my eyes.

'I'm sorry to hear about your husband,' she says, not opening the door fully.

'I'm sorry I never said the same about yours,' I say.

'Old news,' she replies.

'How did you move on?' I ask.

I can sense Mrs Evermoor around us somewhere, watching. I imagine she's thinking to herself: *ah, she's curious. It's working.* Maybe they have one like her in every neighbourhood. Like in the olden days they used to have reps coming to your door to sell you stuff, like double glazing or insurance. Now it's husbands.

'Shall I come around to yours?' Melissa says.

Before I can protest and tell her that my house is an absolute bombsite, she hollers upstairs to Mike that she's going out and starts padding over to my front door in her slippers. As I follow her, I catch sight of Mrs Evermoor in my peripheral vision, pretending to be clipping her hedge with secateurs.

'I'll call round later!' she shouts after us, 'I've got some strawberry and chicken filo parcels on the go!'

I expect Melissa to be shocked by what she finds inside. It's surely the house of a woman who's lost her mind; plates stacked up high in the kitchen, waiting to topple. Clothes are strewn everywhere, as a result of me stuffing all Lloyd's clothes in bin bags and then changing my mind and emptying them all over the floor again. A line of empty wine bottles stand guard at the bifold doors, one for every sorry evening since the day he died. There are also stacks and stacks of teabags that have overflown from the top of the food bin to congeal into a furry little mess, which looks like it's evolving into a new creature. Yet Melissa's curiously calm as she looks at all this, as if it's normal.

She gets me to sit down next to her and takes my hand in hers.

'This is how I was,' she says. 'Right at the beginning.'

It makes me feel bad to hear her saying this, recalling a joke Lloyd and I used to have about her. Didn't we call her the dressing gown lady? That must have been around the time she was in the pit of despair, and there we were, finding her funny.

'I'm sorry I never saw your pain,' I say.

She shakes her head and smiles.

'It's fine,' she says. 'We've never really been friends, never really spoken, have we? Apart from the odd hello. It would have been a bit strange if you'd suddenly tried to be my friend, just because I'd lost someone. Like that suddenly made me someone you had to talk to, couldn't ignore anymore. Almost as if it made me more appealing. You know?'

I feel guilty about it, but she's right. I must have known we were a similar kind of age, and could have become friends, but must have been thinking to myself, *oh well, I've got Lloyd and I've got my friends and I don't need anybody else in my life right now, I'm pretty full up already.* Only throwing a quick smile at her as I was reversing out of my drive. I probably had a better relationship with my side mirror.

'Thing is,' she says. 'My husband wasn't all

that kind to me. He was a drinker, and he was violent sometimes…'

'Did he see other women, too?' I blurt out. I'm still thinking about that postcard, the words *can't wait to see you again* in that childish scrawl.

'No,' she says quietly. 'I was the only one for him. But it was too much at times, you know? Suffocating. His death was a blessing, of sorts.'

It makes me uncomfortable to hear her talk of a death like a blessing. Lloyd's death was anything but. It was the opposite. A curse. A condemnation. Something dreadful to live with for the rest of my life.

'But you know,' she continues. 'I still had a daughter. Who needed a father.'

This stings a bit, I must admit. We had been talking about trying for a baby, just before Lloyd started complaining of a sore throat.

'I never thought it would work,' she says. 'But it did, for me, for us. The new Mike is kind. And thoughtful. And has never touched a drop of alcohol in his life. He loves my little girl Lily like she's his own and there's another' – she pats her belly – 'there's another one on the way now. Which is going to bond Lily and I and him forever.'

'But what are they,' I blurt out, 'these

replacements? I mean, are they genetically engineered or what? Kept in a centre until they come of age? What? What are they? How can they come from nowhere? How can a grown man be from nowhere at all?'

Melissa's face suddenly goes very serious.

'You have to get past that attitude, or they won't let you in the front door,' she says.

'Well Lloyd would want me to ask!'

Lloyd was what they call a futurologist, someone who worked out how things were going to be in ten, twenty, thirty years' time. He spent his life imagining possible, probable and preferable futures. Admittedly, none of those futures included dying at twenty-six from cancer.

'Listen to me,' Melissa says, making me look right into her eyes. 'If you want this, you must accept that some people do come from nowhere. It's the only way.'

I look up at Melissa. I remember her now, scared and alone on her front lawn as my headlights used to sweep over her. I remember running into the house and telling Lloyd, giggling, that the 'dressing gown lady's out there again'. I remember how we'd only talk about her for two minutes and then we'd be making dinner and chatting and drinking wine and doing anything and everything but thinking about why Melissa was out there on the lawn in the first place.

She's a different Melissa now. She's smartly dressed. She looks younger, more beautiful, because she accepted an alternative that's brought her back from the brink of madness.

I will become known as the pyjama lady, I think. Unless I do something about it.

Chapter 4

The Replacement Centre doesn't look like I expect it to; it's a small, oblong building with a flat roof and no windows. I open the door and am greeted with the waft of terrifying times long forgotten about: job interviews, indoor sports, a piano exam.

'Mrs Denton?' asks the woman at reception.

At first I don't recognise my own name. Lloyd and I had only been married for six months when he died, and because by then I knew that his name was the only part of him I could keep, it seemed rude not to take it. I used to rant and rave at Lloyd about how unjust it was that women were made to disappear in this way when they got married; not searchable anymore online, as if they never existed. And yet now I find my invisibility soothing, because even though everyone in my hometown knows what has happened to me, no one on social media knows that Mrs Denton's husband has died.

I am guided into a small room where a red-haired woman with rather frightening blue eyes tells me to sit and relax. She asks me how I heard about the Replacement Centre, so I tell her about the magazine programme and the countless adverts I've seen.

'Can you tell us why you'd benefit from having a replacement?' she asks, as if she's talking about a fridge freezer.

I tell her I'm worried about my lack of movement, of contact with the outside world, my lack of feeling about anything. I tell her I think I need someone to take care of, or someone to take care of me.

She asks me to sign some papers. The form tells me that I have thirty days to change my mind about the replacement. After that time, if I don't want him, I have to bring him back. All replacements are tagged, she tells me, which enables them to be located by the Centre, should they try to escape.

I follow the woman into a darker room, which has a window facing into another room, like in those police procedurals I sometimes watch when I've had enough of all the other programmes. Despite the violence, I find those kinds of programmes quite soothing, because there are no real surprises, however much they try to throw them at you. There's a bad guy, and at some point they'll find out who it is. That's the kind of predictability we'd all like in life, isn't it? But life isn't like that.

I don't know I'm crying until the woman hands me a tissue, the same tissue I'm meant to be able to throw away when all this is done, according to the advert.

'It's normal,' she says, placing a hand on my shoulder. 'This sort of reaction.'

'It is?' I say.

'People think it's some sort of mail-order bride thing,' she says. 'It isn't that at all. It's about giving these people new life. Doing something good.'

This surprises me. How can me coming here, plucking a man at random to fill my life, be a good act?

'How are we doing something for *them*?' I ask.

'Just a manner of speaking,' she says. I see her trying to remain calm, all the while thinking that maybe she shouldn't have said that. 'It's all about goodness, whichever way you look at it.'

Somewhere in the back of my mind I'm remembering Lloyd telling me that the government will find a way of dealing with the problem of immigration by making it feel as though it benefits us, rather than taking away our choices in life. The replacements, I suddenly realise, don't come from nowhere. They come from other countries, from places that have become too dangerous to live in, countries where they aren't free to be themselves. They have come here hoping for a better life and somehow have ended up agreeing to let someone else decide what a better life should be.

'They'll be advertising them on TV,' I remember Lloyd saying. 'Treating them like commodities. Like a spa day, or a new beauty treatment, giving you the impression that it would pave the way for a brand-new you.'

I remember laughing hard about it, this notion of brainwashing the public into accepting such a thing. The idea of me replacing Lloyd with a stranger. The concept of a government being able to advertise people, like they were products.

'Oh, come on! That will never happen,' I said.

'It will,' he said, in that I'm-right-about-this voice of his. 'It will.'

I wonder what Lloyd would say if he could see me now. Sitting at this desk, waiting to be taken into the next room, where I get to choose my replacement for him. All because I looked long and hard at the television and at those tailored ads on my phone and because I'm weak enough to buy into it all, even though I was warned.

He never thought I'd see that postcard, though, did he? Or read the words of the woman who couldn't wait to see him again.

That part of the future he didn't see coming at all.

Chapter 5

A light comes on in the room we're observing through the window. Men begin to filter in. They all look uncannily like Lloyd in one way or another; so much so that it makes my heart soar with hope. *He's here*, I think, even though I know someone dragged me away from his bed and that I saw him laid out at the morgue and that I sat sobbing at the side of his grave for two hours in the pouring rain.

'Can they see me?' I ask, feeling suddenly exposed.

'Not unless you want them to,' the woman replies. 'We have a button we press if the client wants to be identified to them, which slowly brings you into focus.'

'That won't be necessary,' I say.

Two men sit together at a table and start talking.

'Do you want audio?' she asks. 'Sometimes it helps with making a decision. To get a better sense of them. Their English is generally very good now.'

I listen to two Lloyds chatting.

'The food here is improving,' one says. 'I think, new chef?'

'I do not want to eat any more,' the other Lloyd says. 'By eating, we are consenting to it. Do you not see that?'

'You have to eat,' the other says. 'Eating is good.'

'I miss the food my wife used to make.'

The woman presses a button and leans forward: 'No mention of wives, please. We've talked about this.'

I turn my gaze towards another Lloyd, who is standing a little to one side, leaning against a wall. He reminds me of the Lloyd I first met on the corridors of our department, who wandered into my room lost, looking for a lecture theatre. I work in a building where the office numbers run consecutively only for so long, and then continue down the other side of the building, which makes no sense at all. The result of this is that it brings many people down past my office with the expectation that they're headed somewhere else. It's strange to think that that's what brought Lloyd to me in the first place, just a badly designed corridor. You'd think a futurologist could have foreseen it, really. Or at least realised that what the whole experience was telling us was that just because you get to thirty-six it doesn't mean you get to be thirty-seven, or any of the ages after that.

The only other Lloyd left in the room is now sitting on the floor with his head in his hands.

'Number seven, look up,' the woman says, pressing a button.

It's a gentler Lloyd, this one. One who has allowed his hair to grow thick and luscious on top of his head, whereas my Lloyd needed to cut his hair with regularity every six weeks, in order to look presentable, he said, though I always preferred it slightly overgrown. It softened the angles of his face, made him look more attractive.

'Number seven, look up,' the woman says again, more firmly.

He's got so many mannerisms that remind me of Lloyd. That's almost more important than looking like him.

'That's the one I want,' I tell the woman.

I go back to the waiting room and wait for what feels like an eternity. When the door finally opens, there he is: my replacement, clutching a bag, ready to go. He doesn't look up at me. I wonder if I'm meant to carry the bag, but he doesn't offer it to me and so I don't.

I just smile and say thank you, to no one in particular, before confirming at the front desk that the rest of the payment will be transferred in thirty days.

That is, if I don't want to return him.

Chapter 6

On the way home he sits with his body twisted ever so slightly away from me, hand on the grab handle, as if I'm driving dangerously, which I am not. In fact, I'm driving as cautiously as ever, as cautiously as I imagine Lloyd would have done when we brought our first child back from hospital.

I wonder if I'm meant to be making conversation, trying to make him feel comfortable with what is happening. I try to see it as he's seeing it, leaving that centre for the first time only to be driven along this dull, grey road, boxed in on either side by a canopy of bare trees throwing their shadows over us. As I indicate to turn into our estate, I wonder if he's thinking of the scenery back home and wondering how he ended up here, being driven into a red-brick cul-de-sac by a woman called Mrs Denton.

When I pull up outside the house, Mrs Evermoor pops up over the hedge like a jack in the box, wipes her hands on her apron and shuffles down towards the car. She's at the driver's window before I can pull the handbrake up. There's no way past her.

'I've been cooking,' she says. 'Jewelled rice. I wasn't sure what sort of one you'd got but Melissa's husband was really into that stuff.'

Before I can answer she's disappeared around the other side of the car and she's prattling on to the replacement about pistachios and pomegranate seeds. He smiles politely at her and nods his head, not unlike Lloyd would. Lloyd was always more tolerant of her than I was. He said we needed to keep on the right side of our neighbours, because you never knew when something devastating like a pandemic or a natural disaster would hit, and they'd be all we had. After he died, I could sort of see his point.

Melissa and her husband are the next spectators to arrive on cue. Thankfully, they stay on the lawn, and just offer welcoming smiles of support – either to me or to him, it's impossible to tell who needs it most in this moment. I'm not sure if I've imagined it, but he actually stops in his tracks when he sees Mike (Replacement Mike). Mrs Evemoor seems to clock this, too, and ushers my replacement off the drive and towards the front door. When

I turn back, I can see Melissa and Replacement Mike arguing in the doorway, Melissa shaking her head.

Mrs Evermoor says she'll leave us to it and return later with the jewelled rice. For once, I don't want her to leave.

'You're not the first to do this,' she says. 'You won't be the last. It doesn't work out for everybody, of course, but when it does, it's wonderful.'

With that she totters off, mumbling to herself about not having enough dried apricots, wondering whether mangoes will do.

When I open the door, something is different. I can't quite tell what it is at first. Then, I realise, it's the atmosphere. It's lighter somehow, more vacant, and that isn't simply because of the tidying and polishing and disinfecting Mrs Evermoor has been doing in my absence.

It's simply that Lloyd really isn't here anymore. Every shred of him I felt around me in the air has evaporated. His spirit has well and truly fled the place. Like he wants nothing to do with this, with us, with me. Like he's sitting over there on Mrs Evermoor's roof looking over at the house, shaking his head, saying: *good god, if this is the future then I'm better off without one.*

Chapter 7

Our wedding photo is the first thing the replacement sees.

'This is him? Your husband?' he asks.

I nod. I don't know what else to say. The resemblance is uncanny, the same dark eyes, the slightly downturned mouth. Yet the replacement's body is lean and muscular, the body Lloyd could have had. A body that might have saved him, I think, though I hate myself for thinking it.

'I'm sorry for your loss,' he says, like he means it. It makes me want to cry. How can this man, this stranger, the one I've just paid for and brought home, be sorry for what has happened to me, when something much worse is happening to him, right now? Then I consider that maybe this is all part of his training, his conditioning. Maybe those millennials line them up, they tell them: *the first thing you do when you enter your new partner's house is tell them how sorry you are for their loss. This will help establish a good, solid, empathetic relationship between you and them.*

'Are you hungry?' I ask. 'Mrs Evermoor won't be long with the jewelled rice.'

He nods his head. I start to panic at the thought of having to eat at a table again, not sprawled halfway across the floor, images flickering above me. I will have to talk. Make conversation. Then again, haven't I done it countless times, at festivals, conferences, weddings? Don't I always find something to say, skirting around the little stuff, families, jobs, interests, until the wine flows and the conversation deepens and becomes easy? But what is there to talk about, if we're both pretending he came from nowhere?

'I'm tired,' he says. 'Can I sleep first?'

I show him to his room: the spare room, where I used to sleep when I was annoyed with Lloyd about something or other. The spare room is where he died, because he didn't think it was fair on me to die in the king-sized bed where there had only ever been happiness and passion and love.

I don't tell the replacement any of this, of course. I just let him place his bag on his new bed and find myself praying that he won't come into my room in the night. And I hate myself for thinking it: because it's the sort of fear that got them locked up in that Centre in the first place. *Put them all in one place. Don't let them near our women. We need to make sure they know how to treat women before we let them become a part of our society.* Line after line of meaningless chatter, vomiting out of our TV sets, filling up the gulf in our heads.

As I leave the room, I catch him staring out of the window, which overlooks Melissa's garden. Replacement Mike is out there, mowing the lawn. Melissa is making a daisy chain with her daughter. You can just make out the bulge of the pregnancy underneath her loose-fitting shirt. My replacement leans his head against the glass and closes his eyes. He's muttering something to himself. Before I can make out what it is, I hear the doorbell ringing. 'That'll be the rice!' I say in a sing-song voice that is completely at odds with the heaviness in my heart.

I find Mrs Evermoor in my kitchen, holding a great big pan of colourful rice which glistens like a trophy.

'That's so kind of you, Mrs Evermoor,' I say. 'So kind.'

She puts the dish down in the centre of the dinner table, looks at me and cups my face in her hands.

'You're the kind one,' she says. 'Exactly the sort of person they should be sending them to.'

For the first time ever, I consider the fact that she doesn't have a husband. I've never cared enough, I suppose, to ask if she had one, and if she did, what happened to him. You just assume that her being a certain age there would have been one at some point, that he would have died, and that she just got used to being on her own. She mentions a grown-up son every now and then, but he's never been to visit her. Not that I would have noticed. Maybe, seeing what me and Melissa are doing, she's wondering if she should have gone for a replacement too? Then again, I assume there aren't all that many oldies to go around.

I sit at the table and take a spoonful of the multicoloured rice, which is the best thing I've tasted in days. I wait for a bit, and then, when he doesn't appear, I spoon more and more it into my mouth and keep shoveling it in until most of it is gone.

I assume that he must have just slept on longer than he meant to. Maybe he thought I'd knock on his door or holler for him to come down, but it was only when I was at the bottom of the stairs that I realised I didn't even know his name.

Chapter 8

He doesn't resurface until the next day, and by then I'm back in front of the TV; half-woman, half-foam-filled-seat-cushion. He asks me if there's any food in the house, and I have to admit to finishing the rice in the early hours of the morning.

He tells me not to worry, that he'll find something.

'Best of luck with that,' I say.

After rummaging around in the kitchen for a bit he asks if it's OK to make a pizza from some filo pastry he defrosted from the freezer, an out-of-date tin of tomatoes and some cheese he found hidden away in an unopened Christmas hamper. I tell him that he's going to give Mrs Evermoor a run for her money. I try my best to imagine it's Lloyd in there, pottering about, and that once the microwave stops whirring everything will ping back into its rightful place and a ready-made Lloyd will appear.

When he comes back into the room and

hands me a slice of pizza, he does actually look so much like Lloyd that my trembling hands can't control themselves and I end up somehow throwing the food onto my lap. The feel of it, a soft, warm, lovingly made thing, is almost too much for me, as though this filo pastry pizza is the newborn that Lloyd and I never had.

As we eat, we watch a programme about people smashing up their homes to build better ones. The replacement is eating his food off a plate Lloyd and I never used, something from a posh twenty-four-piece set that my auntie bought us when we moved in. They always seemed too good to use for ourselves, we were waiting for some occasion or other, for someone or something better. Crockery for the future. A future in which my Lloyd is dead and buried and a fake Lloyd sits opposite me in my lounge like it's the most natural thing in the world.

'So people destroy their own houses here,' he says, trying to follow what's happening on the TV.

'Yes, to make them better,' I say.

'Lucky them,' he says.

Once we're finished he picks up my plate and disappears into the kitchen with it. I hear him washing the dishes, moving things, putting things away. The sort of stuff a normal person does, the kind of simple stuff I've been unable to do all these months.

'What are we going to do today?' he says, popping his head back through the door frame, tea towel draped over his shoulder like a feather boa.

Lloyd and I used to joke that the reason we got on so well was because we never felt inclined to be the kind of couple that wanted to *do things*. That we were perfectly fine not walking around castles, visiting Victorian follies or going out for a pub lunch. We were happy to spend Saturdays lazing in bed, eating toast, reading the papers, making love. Then, when that came to an end, we were fine spending the rest of our free time working, in separate rooms, taking each other cups of tea. We liked to work. But you don't take pictures of people working, do you? Now I think we should have spent less time at the desk, and certainly less time in bed. I remember my grandmother's mantra all too well: *people die in bed, you know.*

I grab the remote and flick through the guide: there are three more hours of this reconstruction programme I could be watching, then something about becoming a top model, then some soap operas. It seems that there's enough here for me not to have to think about anything else for the rest of the day and this is how I want it. I want him to do that too, but I can't bring myself to say it.

'We could go for a walk, maybe?' he says. I nod my head. I imagine the millennials encircling him: *everything you do has to be decided by your new owner. If they want to watch TV, you watch TV. If they want to go out, you must go out. You must do things together.*

'What do I call you?' I say, without looking up. I think of the fact that the replacement next door is still called Mike. No one calls him 'Replacement Mike', except for me.

'They said you get to decide,' he says, switching channels without asking if it's okay. He puts on a cartoon, where a little squirrel dashes up a tree and hides from a bear. It's the sort of thing I'd never watch, but he seems engrossed. He laughs, the laugh gone just as quickly as it appears, as if he's used to someone telling him to stop. *Don't appear too happy*, the millennials might have said. *These people will be very sad, it's important to be considerate of their feelings.*

'Well, what is your name?' I ask. I can't imagine it would ever be possible to call him Lloyd.

'Ali,' he says.

'Well then that's what we'll call you, Ali,' I say.

I know that if I think too much about going outside I won't do it, so I don't get changed, I just hoist some boots on and open the front door and step out. Ali follows, and once we're out in the brash sunlight, what seemed so simple only minutes before now seems complicated. Do I hold his hand? His arm in mine? How is this supposed to work? I imagine all my neighbours are standing behind the thin film of their net curtains right now, wanting to see how it will all unfold. The pressure to perform just becomes too much, and I feel weak and faint, desperate to return to the house. In the end he grabs hold of my elbow to stop me from falling backwards and we shuffle onwards awkwardly, one step at a time, with him looking more like my carer than my husband.

We manage a few small steps around the cul-de-sac, *baby steps*, the grief counsellor would have said, and then turn around to come back, by which time Mrs Evermoor is pressure-washing the life out of her driveway, just so she can get a good look at us. Above the stream of water she shouts at us: 'Was thinking of having a barbecue this evening if you fancy it?'

I don't fancy it, any more than I fancied being outdoors in the first place, but then I think about having to spend the evening alone with Ali.

'We'll be there,' I say, forcing a weak smile. 'Won't we, Ali?'

Mrs Evermoor seems surprised I'm not calling him Lloyd, but tries her best to hide it.

'Ali,' she repeats. 'Well, now then, isn't that a nice name? Do you like lamb skewers with minted tzatziki, Ali?'

He tells me he thinks I should take a shower before the barbecue. I find it insulting at first, but then I look in the mirror and see his point. I haven't been washing all that much lately, scared that a layer of soap, a dab of perfume, would wash away the last of Lloyd. Also, I haven't been in the en-suite shower room since Lloyd became ill, because that was the last place he bathed and washed and cried hard, and so I just sit outside the door for a while, breathing in my own sweat and grime. Ali steps over me eventually, turns the dial of the shower for me and leaves the hot water running for long enough that the steam sets off the smoke alarm. I disappear into the mist that's flowing towards me from the bathroom, arms outstretched like a magician, hoping I'll never return.

When I come out in my towel, he's standing there at the top of the landing with a strange look on his face, as if he's nervous about something.

'Do you want to...um...you know?' he says, gesturing towards the bedroom. I see from his eyes that he doesn't want to, not at all, any more than I do.

'Oh god, no,' I say. 'No, absolutely not.'

'That's OK then,' he says. 'I have to offer to go to bed with you within twenty-four hours of coming here, I hope you understand.'

Melissa and replacement Mike are at the barbecue and I watch them with a renewed interest, thinking of Mike offering himself up to Melissa like Ali just did to me. Melissa obviously took him up on his offer straight away, if that bulge underneath her blouse is anything to go by.

'We're all glad to see you getting on with your life,' Melissa says, handing me a kebab.

'Is that what this is, then?' I say. 'Getting on with life?'

'Well, what else is it?' she asks.

'A distraction,' I say. 'I'm not keeping him, I just thought it would be good to try something out.'

'That's what everyone says at first,' she says.

Ali and Mike don't talk much during the barbecue at all, which I find a little strange, but maybe it's uncomfortable for them to have to acknowledge each other. Maybe it's presumptuous for us to expect 'these types', as Mrs Evermoor refers to them, to get on, just because they've come from the same centre. They both seem to be enjoying themselves, however, and keep smiling through the whole awkward affair, helping Mrs Evermoor with the barbecue, turning the sizzling pieces of meat, refilling glasses. Mrs Evermoor seems in her element with these two big men fussing around her, and the evening passes in a bit of a blur, with me sitting on the grass drinking Pimms while Melissa's little girl dances around me. I keep thinking that if I drink enough and squint in the sun I can pretend that everything is as it should be. I can tell myself that it's Lloyd over there, helping Mrs Evermoor. A new Lloyd who wants to do things, go out and meet people. A new Lloyd who now knows that you can't take every moment for granted and shouldn't be sitting at your computer with your head buried in a book about a future you won't see.

I must have had a little too much to drink,

because the next thing I know I've made the little girl cry because I've told her that some people just aren't meant to be daddies and that lies will kill you in the end. I'm talking about Lloyd, because I keep remembering the postcard and thinking that maybe he was going to leave me anyway, but she somehow thinks I'm talking about her dad, replacement Mike. I try to make things better by telling her she's got a much nicer dad now than the one she had before, and the next thing I know Ali is scooping me up off the grass, lifting me up and carrying me towards the gate. Replacement Mike and Melissa seem to have disappeared in a puff of barbecue smoke.

'All we want is a person who can scoop us up off the floor when it all gets a bit much,' I can hear Mrs Evermoor saying, somewhere far, far away.

As he places me down on the bed, he hovers awhile in the room, pacing back and forth. He's probably wondering if he should offer to sleep with me again but wondering if I'm in a fit state to make the right decision. I think about Lloyd making the same decision about the person who couldn't wait to see him again, that person in the other country, that he probably met on one of his conferences.

I think about the fact that there have been no other postcards, no phone calls. No one wondering why they are not seeing him again.

Whoever sent that postcard wanted me to know about her. She must have done.

Chapter 9

The next morning the woman from the Replacement Centre rings me to run through what she calls 'maintenance enquiries'.

'How's it all going?' she says cheerily, pretending to be my friend.

'OK, I guess,' I say. 'I got a bit drunk last night and made a fool of myself.'

'Is he fitting in with your routine?'

I tell her that my routine consists of sitting in front of the TV, watching homes being smashed up or listening to people talking nonsense on brightly coloured sofas.

'And does he also enjoy that?' she asks.

Ali doesn't watch TV with me anymore; instead, he mooches about the house, reads some of Lloyd's books, sits at Lloyd's desk. I find it increasingly difficult to get absorbed in my programmes. You can't really slob around comfortably with someone else in the house.

'Hello, are you there?'

For some reason, I lie, and tell the lady yes,

he sits with me, watches TV with me, eats with me; that he does what I do. I feel that if I were to answer in any other way, it might pave the way for other questions that I don't have the patience to answer.

'You don't find any of his activities disturbing, alarming, or a cause for concern?'

I tell her that one day I walked into Lloyd's study to find Ali reading one of Lloyd's history books and thought it was odd he was taking an interest in my dead husband's work.

'Reading, ok, I'll note that,' she says, without emotion. 'Ok, but there's nothing more than that? Nothing you feel would warrant surveillance?'

'Unless you want to study how he puts the bins out,' I say. 'He hasn't quite got it up to the standard of Replacement-Mike-Next-Door.'

'Ok, no surveillance necessary,' she says, moving swiftly on. 'And finally, has the relationship been consummated?'

'No,' I say abruptly.

I wonder, as she click-clacks my answer onto the screen, if there's a right way to answer these questions. I wonder if there's some special note being attached to my application: *no sex yet, looks unlikely to keep him.*

'Thank you for your time,' she says, ending the call before I have a chance to say anything else.

I should have told her that one thing that's making me feel on edge is that I don't see any adverts about the Replacement Centre anymore, which makes me paranoid that they are somehow watching me through the screen. *Look how well we did!* the millennials are saying. *We made her take one! One less for us to worry about!*

I turn the TV off and listen out for him. He's still in Lloyd's study I think, and so I hoist myself up off the sofa to go and look for him. As I approach the door, the stillness unnerves me. All sorts of thoughts run through my mind: what if I'm going to find him dead, like Lloyd. Lloyd's death was pretty abrupt in the end, and I know it sounds stupid, but even though I know it was coming, I didn't see it coming. He was well enough to ask for a cup of soup, but by the time I'd returned with it, gone. Just like that.

I open the door slowly and cautiously and find Ali hunched at the computer. He looks up guiltily at me before shutting down the screen, but not before I've seen that he was trying to email someone, in a language where the letters are all loops and dots, so they don't even look like letters to me.

'How... how did you get into that?' I ask. Not

even I, his wife, was ever allowed access to that computer. Even now, I haven't been able to guess his password, and the software companies are useless in trying to help get around it. 'We are loyal to our customers, even in death,' one of them said to me over the phone.

'There are always ways around a password,' he says. 'I've set it now so that anyone can use it. Anytime.'

'Oh, OK, and is that allowed? I mean, are you allowed to do things like that?'

'We're allowed to do what you allow us to do,' he says.

I think again about what the woman said on the phone: *nothing you think would warrant surveillance?* I imagine with one phone call, a click of a button, they could access Lloyd's computer and find out exactly who it is that Ali's emailing, and why. Something about the sadness in his eyes when he looks up makes me think of Lloyd, in those final days where the chemo was no longer working and he knew his time was up.

'Just carry on doing what you need to do,' I tell him, and leave the room. I hear him open the laptop again and hammer away at the keyboard like his life depends on it.

Later that evening, when Ali's asleep, I go to the computer and open it up. I click on the mouse pad and the room lights up suddenly as the screensaver comes into view. It's a picture of me and Lloyd on holiday, arms wrapped around each other. The picture used to make me so happy, and I almost can't bear seeing it now. At least he still loved me enough to keep it as his screensaver.

The desktop is suspiciously clean, the odd file dotted here and there containing some of his notes and lectures.

And then, just as I'm about to log off, I notice one file just titled 'R'. I click on it and a notification comes up saying the file is encrypted. I think about the postcard and wonder what this file could possibly contain that would warrant an encryption. Nudes? Pictures of them in bed together? I click on it again. Ali, surely, will know how to get around something like this. I holler out his name – 'Ali! Ali?' – but no one comes.

I rush to the bedroom and find him fast asleep, thrashing around on the bed. He looks frenzied, sweating profusely, trapped in some kind of terrible nightmare.

And he's whispering names to himself: *Amena, Ousa, Rasha*, over and over again.

I go back to bed and wonder about them, this Amena, Ousa, Rasha, and where they might be right now. Whether they know their names are being called out in darkness by someone who, by the sounds of it, feels their absence like a physical pain.

I close down the computer and decide that I don't want to know anything about that file. At least not yet.

Chapter 10

The next day, Melissa calls round. Her belly's grown a few inches in the last few days and she's breathing heavily. I take her through to the kitchen and get her a glass of water, while Ali disappears upstairs.

'Has he been different, these last few days?' Melissa asks, panting.

'What do you mean?'

'Restless?'

I think of the cries in the middle of the night. The more he cries out for them, the more I think Amena, Ousa, Rasha might no longer be alive. I've been wondering if for my one loss, he might actually have suffered three. Not that it's a competition.

'I suppose a little bit, yes,' I say. 'He's been using Lloyd's computer.'

Melissa looks concerned.

'He's not allowed to do that, surely,' she says. 'Mike still hasn't been given his own device to use, not since he got here.'

'Can't see it doing much harm,' I say, 'and anyway, it was him who sorted out the problem of getting into it. There's something on there... that... I think Lloyd didn't want me to see.'

'Like what?' she asks.

'I think he was seeing someone, before he got ill,' I say, as the truth of it hits me deep in the stomach. 'I think he was probably going to leave me.'

'Well, you can't trust one of them if you ask me, not unless you're the one calling the shots, like we are now. Society would fare much better if the women did the choosing and the men weren't allowed to run away.'

She looks off into the far distance as I try to absorb what she's just said. The Replacement Centre have done a proper job on her. She's completely brainwashed.

'Anyway, there is definitely something odd going on,' Melissa continues, rubbing her belly.

'What do you mean?' I ask.

'Since your replacement arrived,' she says, 'Mike's been acting odd. Like he's... angry about something.'

'Well, it might have brought a few things back to him,' I say. What I don't say is that maybe it's woken Mike up to the fact that getting Melissa pregnant and buying into all this happy family nonsense was never a good idea.

'He's been very secretive,' she says. 'Sneaking around at bedtime. Going out into the garden at odd hours, staring over at your house. I wondered if Ali was doing the same?'

Ali no longer has to email in secret. I allow him as much access to the computer as he wants now, and he seems happier for it. Sometimes he has the occasional Zoom with someone, and I hear him laughing; big, guttural laughs unlike anything I've heard before. I wonder if somehow Mike has found out about this. That he knows that Ali has all this access to things, that he has the freedoms of a normal person, that I'm a different kind of partner to Ali than Melissa is to him. More like a partner-in-crime. Not that I'm sure what crime it is I'm committing just yet, or what the repercussions of it will be.

'No, not really,' I say. 'But I'll keep an eye on him.'

That night I stay up late watching some awful drama set in a café where a woman keeps cooking elaborate desserts late at night to make herself feel better about being dumped by her boyfriend. I'm only half watching it, because there's a much more interesting drama to be seen from my window, which is that of Melissa and Replacement Mike arguing in their garden.

I can't hear what they're saying, but Melissa keeps pointing over at my house and shaking her head. I decide to go up to the study to see what Ali is up to, but he's nowhere to be seen. I walk in and out of rooms, calling out his name, but he doesn't come. I push open the door to his bedroom and his bed is perfectly made. Lloyd's books are on the bedside table. It takes my breath away and makes me think, for the first time since Ali came here, that Lloyd might be back.

From here I can see all across the sprawl of lawns that connect our little cul-de-sac. Melissa and Mike are still arguing, and Melissa is crying by now. I imagine the script, Melissa saying *you're not the same anymore* or *I want my Mike back*, by which she actually means she wants the Replacement Mike back, and not the old drunken one who used to bash her about. I imagine Mike is saying, *I miss my old life too* or *Ali doesn't have to pretend to be anything he's not, why should I?*

I go back into Lloyd's study and sit down at the desk in the darkness. The computer is still whirring as it hasn't been turned off properly. I try to shut it down but a notification tells me I can't shut the computer down until I've quit Zoom. I notice a small dialogue box is open at the side of the computer, and to my surprise, I notice that the Zoom meeting Ali was having hasn't actually finished.

I click on the dialogue box. Through the screen I am transported to an ordinary kind of living room, a pretty old fashioned one with floral upholstery. I recognise it, but can't immediately identify where it is.

Suddenly I sense a presence behind me. It's Ali, who tells me he's sorry if I couldn't find him, he was planting some kale in the garden. He sees what I'm looking at and he seems worried all of a sudden, trying to get me to come away from the screen by promising to come down and watch TV with me, apologising for being such a recluse.

'What is this? Who have you been talking to?' I ask him, still not able to make sense of what I'm seeing in front of my eyes.

'It's not what you think,' Ali says, before I even know what I think.

We both turn back to look at the screen, and before long a face comes into the frame. The unmistakable face of my neighbour, Mrs Evermoor.

'Ali? How do I turn this thing off? Do you know?' she asks.

And with that Ali slams the laptop shut.

Chapter 11

Ali tells me he was just asking Mrs Evermoor for some of her recipes. When I say that he could have done that over the garden fence he stutters and rubs his face and seems uncomfortable.

'I didn't want you to think I was spending too much time over there, and not with you,' he says.

None of it makes sense. What does make sense is that Mrs Evermoor is far more involved in this scheme than I first thought. Perhaps she's more than a rep. She could be like some kind of probation officer, making sure they're keeping on the right track.

I need to tell Melissa. Mrs Evermoor waves at me as I cross the path in front of her house and asks if I want to try some sweet potato brownies.

'No thank you,' I say.

'Don't blame you, they are a bit dense,' she says. 'Oh, are you going to visit Melissa? I wouldn't right now. She's having a hard time with that pregnancy, bless her.'

I want to ask her if she knows all this from snooping at her through her webcam, but I stop myself. I can't let Mrs Evermoor know I'm onto her, or god knows what would be reported back to the agency, or where that would leave my poor Ali.

My poor Ali. I'm starting to think of him, rather worryingly, as mine. As my property. Like a comfort blanket or a pet. And I know that's wrong, but it's working, isn't it, this scheme of theirs? The voice-over of the advert suddenly comes back to me – *throw away your tissues* – and I realise that I haven't cried for days. I don't even think I have any tissues in the house to throw away. Slowly, steadily, all my grief seems to have dried up.

Melissa seems pale and withdrawn when she comes to the door and insists it's just the tricky last trimester with the baby that's bringing on some horrible migraines and bloating. She says she's resting, that Mike and her daughter are out, because she wanted some time to herself. I know it's a hint that I shouldn't come in, but I desperately need to escape Mrs Evermoor's gaze now.

'Feeling a bit faint myself to be honest,' I say, starting to sway a little against her front door, 'could I just…'

Before she's had time to protest I'm at the kitchen sink guzzling down some water. Like clockwork, Mrs Evermoor moves into her back garden, where she's pretending to be tending to her green beans but ever so slyly watching the kitchen window through her cataract glasses. I pull down the blinds without asking Melissa's permission.

'What are you doing?' she asks.

'Bit bright in here,' I say. 'Sure it doesn't help with the migraines.'

I turn and look at Melissa.

'You were right,' I say quietly. 'There is something odd going on. It's Mrs Evermoor, isn't it? She's watching them?'

Melissa looks at me now and nods her head. With the light falling in stripes across her pale face, she looks like a woman in pieces, desperate to become whole again. She sits down and looks up earnestly at me and bursts into tears.

'I think she suspects Mike's planning to leave,' she says. 'And she's trying to stop him. But she doesn't have the proof.'

'And you do?' I ask.

'I found some documents. It's all a ruse, isn't it, all this? They play the game, they come to us, pretend to love us, and then, when they're all legitimate and legal, they can move on. We're not in control of any of it, really.'

I think of Ali, alone in Lloyd's room. I'm not sure how I imagined it would all end, really, but I wasn't planning on marrying him or having his baby. Or was I? I feel a pang now, thinking that this could be the only chance I have. Maybe these men think this is how everyone gets what they want. We get the baby we can't have because our husbands are dead, and they get the documentation they need to move on.

'Tell Mrs Evermoor then,' I say. 'Give her the documents.'

Melissa stares at me blankly.

'I don't know. I don't know what the punishment is for this kind of thing.'

'Surely she'll just make sure he stays with you...'

'What if she doesn't?' she says. 'What if she gets him killed?'

I open the blinds. I can see Mrs Evermoor poised with her hand loper, tending to her rhododendron bush.

I find myself wondering how a woman like that came to hold all the power.

Chapter 12

Melissa and I decide to do nothing, for the time being, except keep a close eye on Mike, an even closer eye than Mrs Evermoor is keeping on him. Melissa also suggests that I should get myself pregnant now, to cement the bond between myself and Ali. To gain back some control.

I find myself thinking about it in earnest. I would like a baby, that much is true. I find myself hovering outside Ali's door at night, willing myself to go in, but then I hear him calling out for Amena, Ousa and Rasha, and I just can't do it.

One morning, Ali makes me walk for longer than I've walked in months. The sun is warm on my face and I feel the blood being pumped all around my body, the oxygen rushing to my brain. Adrenalin whirls inside me. I try to see us from a distance as other people do: man and wife, out strolling in this happy green place, a no-kids-yet couple who have delusions of grandeur about the future.

Yet our future is only fourteen more days, unless I decide otherwise.

He takes me for a coffee in a little deli I've always walked past in a rush, orders pastries and we sit there eating them.

'In fourteen days, you're going to take me back,' he says.

'Not necessarily,' I say.

'But you don't want me,' he says. 'Do you?'

'It depends what you mean by want,' I say.

'They only let us stay if it works,' he says. 'If you keep me they'll come out to see us, they'll assess you. Assess me. Ask whether or not we are going to have children. There's a process. You think they'll let me stay just cooking your food and reading your husband's books?'

'Amena, Ousa, Rasha,' I say. 'Who are they?'

He looks stunned. I wonder if he's surprised I know their names, or surprised that I care.

'Amena was my wife. Ousa and Rasha were our children.'

'Were?' I say. 'They're dead?'

'I think so. There was an explosion, the whole house...' His voice starts to tremble. I hold his hand and encourage him to finish the story. Funny how, when you've experienced so much grief yourself, you know how to guide someone else through it. 'The whole house caved in on us. I was dragged out, put on a truck... next thing I know I'm at the Replacement Centre. I think I was maybe traumatised, or brain damaged or something. I wouldn't have left them behind if I'd have known what I was doing.'

'So what's your plan?' I say. Lloyd said everyone had to have a plan.

'I can give you a child if you want,' he says. 'I am happy, if I can do that for you.

I know it's what you want. What you need. Maybe.'

'And in exchange?' I ask. I know, from the way he says it, that there will be some kind of trade off.

'Once the baby is born, I want to go and find them. Find out what happened to them.'

I find myself jealous, all of a sudden, that he still has a glimmer of hope in all this. I imagine that my Lloyd isn't gone, that he was just lying under some rubble all along. That he was pulled out and saved. Then I realise how ridiculous it is for me to be jealous of a man who had his whole life destroyed in one second and found himself sold off to be part of a different family.

'But how will you get past Mrs Evermoor?' I venture.

He looks up.

'What do you mean?'

'Isn't she there to stop you?' I ask. 'Don't they make sure that there are these officers everywhere, these intelligence agents, there to watch your every move, people like her, who look like ordinary people, so that you can't escape?'

Now he seems even more surprised. I see it a fraction of a second before he says it; the likeness between them.

'No, she's there to help me,' he says. 'She was a replacement too. She also happens to be my mother.'

Chapter 13

Ali tells me that Mrs Evermoor's real name is Abreshima. It means 'made of silk', Ali tells me, which doesn't really suit her, because he says she's actually made of much stronger stuff. More like steel. He tells me how Abreshima was a journalist by trade, and how she wrote lots and lots of things that criticised their country's government, but that she went a little bit too far with it sometimes. After a while, she realised that her life was in danger. To keep safe, she went to live in the mountains, but when Ali went up there to visit her one day with Ousa and Rasha he found the door wide open and no one home. He assumed they had thrown her in prison, but he couldn't find any record of her, no matter how many prisons he traipsed around, trying to get information. More and more journalists during that time were disappearing from their homes, he said, and quietly it seemed that they would just have to accept that they'd been killed. But something told Ali that Abreshima wouldn't be dead. He could feel it deep inside.

'She was a fighter. She had this way with words, a way of getting out of things,' he tells me. 'Saying the right things, winning every argument. She could be whoever she needed to be in any given moment, just to save herself.'

When Ali's own home was bombed a few months later and he found himself on that truck, and then in the Centre, it struck him that this might have been what happened to his mother too. When his cellmate, Replacement Mike, was selected by Melissa, Mike promised to send back any information he could regarding his mother. What Ali hadn't expected was that Mike ended up living next door to Abreshima, who he recognised instantly from the one remaining picture of the whole family that Ali had been allowed to keep, pasted on the wall of his room. Mike didn't approach her, but soon found that she was around the house a lot, cooking for them, encouraging their union. She had said something cryptic to him one day about his relationship with Melissa being 'a good way out', and he had realised she was telling him subtly that he should try to make the union a success, for his own good. Because, rumour had it, if your owner didn't decide to keep you, you had less of a chance of being put up for selection again. You could well end up staying in the Replacement Centre for the rest of your days.

Mike had tried his best with Melissa, even though he was wracked with guilt about starting afresh with someone new. He, too, had left a family behind, a wife and son, never knowing what happened to them. He had a lot of anger inside him that he didn't quite understand, which meant he always acted up whenever he was called to 'parade' for those looking for a replacement. No one ever chose him. After a while, however, he began to think that the only way of finding out what had happened to his family was to get out, and to try somehow to make contact with back home. When Melissa walked in, looking lost and bruised and looking like she wouldn't expect much from anyone, just a bit of care and attention, he made sure to be on his best behaviour and before he knew it he was mowing Melissa's front lawn.

Mike wasn't sure if he should try to approach Mrs Evermoor. She seemed like such an ordinary little woman, and she certainly wasn't showing any signs of being anything other than your average next door neighbour.

'My mother knows how to keep safe, you

see,' Ali continues. 'When to make your move, when to lay low. But she would leave little clues for Mike. She would make dishes that were unique to his country, his culture. They didn't taste like someone trying to follow some exotic recipe, they tasted like the real thing. So he knew that what she was telling him, through all this food, was that, yes, I am who you think I am. And I'm here to help.'

Eventually, Ali said, Mike and Mrs Evermoor started to talk, late at night, out in the garden. In their own language, through a hole in the fence. Mike told her he'd met a man who he thought was her son. Abreshima told him she knew how to make contact with people in his hometown, but that he'd have to be patient, get past the probation period and get himself a device that the Replacement Centre wouldn't know how to trace.

I tell Ali to stop, that I don't want to hear anymore. I've worked the rest of it out for myself, I say. How Abreshima, after her huge success with Mike, started to hear rumours that Lloyd was ill. How she pretended to care, bringing dishes over while Lloyd was at the hospital. Then seeing him come home, and seeing the palliative carers come and go. Preparing herself for the big moment when

Lloyd would go and her son could be brought back to her. I imagine her rubbing her hands together gleefully, rejoicing at the fact that there would soon be an 'opening' next door, a hole where my heart used to be.

'No, no,' Ali says, when I share this with him, 'you must not think like that, that's not how it was.'

I'm angry now, because it seems that this is exactly how it was. It seems like they've been playing us, all three of them, from the very beginning.

'Listen to me,' Ali says. 'Abreshima would never have been happy to hear that Lloyd was dying. Lloyd was a good man. She liked him...'

'She hardly knew him!' I realise I am crying now, big, huge, ugly sobs, springing from somewhere that's been shut down for too long. And now I need my tissues, desperately, and so the woman on the advert lied, I think, because look at me. *Look at me.* The people in the deli are all staring, and as I look around me and see these perfect couples, I wonder how many of them are the real thing, and how many are, in fact, replacements?

I leave the deli and run back through the park we walked through shortly before, the place where I had almost convinced myself that

I was happy. I suddenly ache for my TV screen, for the fictional hotel rooms I closed myself off in, for the sofa on which nobody told the truth. It seems so much easier than confronting my reality; a reality in which nothing seems real at all.

Chapter 14

I go back into the house and run upstairs into the spare bedroom. I try to piece it together in my mind, how Mrs Evermoor, Abreshima, was the original replacement. But where has Mr Evermoor gone, the man who presumably chose her? Could he be buried under her rhododendron bush? Is that what they are planning to do to me, if I don't end up agreeing with their plans?

I start picking up Ali's things and hurling them into a bag. I feel so angry to have been used like this, for my life and my grief to have been seen just as a vehicle for bringing another family back together, when my own chance at a family with Lloyd is gone. I could get them into serious trouble, I think – Ali, Mike, Abreshima – get them sent back to the Replacement Centre for the remainder of their days. As I hurl Ali's stuff into bags and pull out his very few possessions, I see it for the first time, the picture of himself with Amena, a curly haired woman with a generous smile. Children of around seven or eight, who I assume to be Ousa and Rasha, are clinging onto his leg, heads thrown backwards, laughing uncontrollably. Standing in the back is a steely, upright Abreshima, so unlike the stooped Mrs Evermoor.

The picture is unmistakably one that shows me a family, a close-knit unit, with Abreshima at the helm. And yet, what remains of this picture? Amena, Ousa and Rasha are no more than names being called out at night, Abreshima and Ali no more than extras in other people's lives.

I try not to think about this too much, because if I start thinking about it, I may feel sorry for them. Feel compassion even. Where was their compassion for me when my husband was dying and it was nothing more to them than a golden opportunity? And yet I also find myself wondering how they did it. I mean, it was one thing them knowing I would lose my husband, but quite another ensuring I would go for a replacement when he died. How could they know I'd choose Ali?

I open another drawer and it catches me off guard. It's full of Lloyd's stuff, stuff I managed never to clear out; paper bills from countries no one visits anymore, half-written postcards, sweet wrappers twisted into golden spirals, receipts scrunched within an inch of their lives, train tickets that were never reclaimed, every moment Lloyd ever lived becoming confetti in my hands. I'm angry at him now, angry for leaving me like he did, and so I start shoving it all into a black bin liner. I don't want any trace of either one of them here, Lloyd or Ali, I just want to start again, but the more I shove these things into the bin, the more I start to see that they aren't just scattered there haphazardly, they are covering something up. A black file that I haven't seen before.

I pull it out. It looks like one of Lloyd's work files, but it seems strange that he kept it by his bedside while he was dying. Maybe he believed if he worked hard enough he wouldn't die. When I open it, I see sheets of paper written in another language, one I do not understand. I wonder whether this is actually Ali's file, because the looping characters look like the ones I've seen him use on the computer. But across them in faint type are the words 'Lloyd Bowen', like the documents were sent specifically to him.

I become aware of a presence in the doorway. It isn't Ali. I would recognise the scent of lavender and garlic and paprika and dahlias anywhere, the scent of a woman who spends a quarter of her life in the kitchen, a quarter in the garden, and the other half of it spying on people through her webcam.

It's Mrs Evermoor. Or should I say Abreshima.

'What are these?' I turn to her and ask her wildly. 'Did you give him paperwork to sign while he was dying? How could you do such a thing?'

'You've misunderstood,' she says, in a steely voice. 'We didn't force Lloyd to do anything he didn't want to do. He wanted to support us.'

'You took advantage of a dying man!' I say, regretting all those times I let Mrs Evermoor into my dying husband's room, just so I could have a bit of respite.

'His illness was unfortunate, yes, but...'

'Unfortunate! That's what you call losing your husband?'

'I mean, that he wasn't able to see his plan through...'

'What do you mean? What plan?'

Abreshima looks at me with surprise.

'This was all Lloyd's idea,' she says. 'He's the one who got us all here.'

Chapter 15

Seems I didn't know Lloyd as well as I thought I did, although I should have seen it coming. Who would have a better handle on the future than a futurologist? And would know how to control it, even in death?

'When I was picked up at the Replacement Centre,' Abreshima says, 'you can imagine how repulsed I was by the whole idea of it. This horrid little man singling me out and then driving me home in the car to some boxed-in neighbourhood of identical red-bricked houses, so unlike my own retreat in the mountains. But when we got there, he told me to wait in the house while he went to get this friend next door, who would know what to do. That friend was Lloyd. You see, Lloyd had read about me, about this journalist who had 'disappeared' and been taken to a different country to try to 'blend in'. When the old lady next door died, he made some kind of deal with the man who lived there, who was around the right sort of age for getting a replacement. He showed him a picture of me, said all he had to do was to choose me, bring me home, decide to keep me, and then he would be free to live his life as he wanted. Lloyd had been keeping a close eye on this man, you see, and all the time his wife was ill he knew he was having an affair with someone else. He went to live with her in some sunny country and told the government he was still living with me.'

My head is spinning.

'There was a postcard...' I say.

'Can't wait to see you again,' Mrs Evermoor says. 'Lloyd asked them to wait a couple of weeks before he died to send that out. It had to come at the right time, or it wouldn't work.'

'He wanted me to have a replacement?' I say. 'He discussed it with you?'

'He knew I had a son, inside the Centre. I'd always joked how alike they looked. He was keen that some good come out of his death. But he knew you wouldn't want to replace him, not at first. Not until you thought maybe he wasn't the person you thought he was. So we came up with that idea about the postcard, because he knew how you'd react to it. He said I could tell you, when the time was right, that it had all been a farce, that he would never have cheated on you. He knew how badly you wanted a child – he said that if you wanted Ali to give you a child, then that's what should happen, as a thank you for everything he'd done for us. That's what needed to happen before Ali and I could move on.'

'Move on?' I say. 'That's the plan?'

'Yes,' she says. 'For me and Ali. Lloyd sorted everything for us. Passports, birth certificates, things to get us back home. It's just, Mike found out... He wants to come with us. He's been making things difficult, saying he'll report us if he doesn't come too. But the thing is, we can't allow him to come. Because the thing is...I recognised Mike when I came here, so did Ali... he was a soldier, not one of us. He's the kind of person who would have killed me, back then...'

'So he's a danger to Mel? Then she needs to know...'

'He isn't a danger to her anymore. I can't say for sure what happened to him. Some kind of head injury, I think. He doesn't remember that he was violent, that he was an aggressor, it's all been knocked out of him. Perhaps by the very explosion that took Ali's family away. Maybe he ended up on the truck by accident. He doesn't remember that he threatened me once, held a gun to my head. He thinks... he thinks he's one of us. And if he stays here, I think he can be, but we can't take him with us...because there will be people who will tell him who he was, and he'll remember...and god knows what he'll turn back into...'

I think of how gentle Mike has been with Melissa. How she loves him. I decide right there and then that she never needs to know who he really is, because he isn't that person anymore.

'We have to move quickly though, with that baby so close to being born – they come out, you see, they assess them, once the baby comes. They always check in on the nearby replacements. And Ali's probation is running out, and I assume, had you wanted a child...'

I think of Ali's rather shy attempts to come into my bedroom. Or rather, hovering outside it, nervously. Lloyd telling them they should at least give me the option of declining. And perhaps it is my only chance, after all. I feel like I'm standing on a very sharp precipice, like I need to jump now, but I don't have the strength to do it.

'I don't have to agree to any of this,' I say, angry now at being played like this. 'I can just take Ali back and be done with it. He has a tag, you know. He can't just...'

'He has the tag until you say you want to keep him, yes,' Abreshima says. 'Then there's a period of fourteen days with no tag, before they come out to check everything is going well. In fourteen days,' she continues, eyes welling up, 'I could be back where I belong. We both could.'

'Do you think Amena, Ousa and Rasha are dead?' I ask.

'Who knows?' she says. 'Sometimes people get lucky. It's the way of things. One day you might live, the next, not.'

'And you want to go back to that, to that fear?'

'I want to be where I belong, not where I'm made to belong,' she says, adding, 'You take your time, dear,' and patting me on the arm. For a moment it seems like she's returned to being Mrs Evermoor. 'Have a good cry, even. But mainly, have a good think. Lloyd wanted his death to be useful. Not many people can think that far ahead, or even care what life meant to anyone once they were gone. But he did. He thought of everything.'

'How can I believe any of this?' I ask.

'I'll prove it to you,' she says.

With that, she walks out of the room, and guides me gently towards Lloyd's study. She clicks on the encrypted file entitled 'R'. She presses a few buttons, a password, and we enter. It doesn't seem anything out of the ordinary, just a file with many documents on it, all with various, unfamiliar names as their heading, but it tells me everything I need to know.

'It's a list of people he was trying to save,' Abreshima says. 'Look, that's where we are, me and Ali, and Mike. But there are so many others he found out about. Ones he was planning to locate with families who would be sympathetic to the cause. But we'll have to delete it now. Delete all data from his computer. Before they come.'

It takes my breath away. This long list of names. Lloyd's intention, all along, was to do good. He knew that I'd eventually see the simplicity in it, that even the R on that postcard stood for REPLACEMENT. A replacement fictional person for him to have an affair with. Just an idea which helped to get me just angry enough to bring Ali home.

I tell Abreshima to copy the file onto a memory stick before she deletes it and that I'll need time to think about the next steps.

Chapter 16

I stay awake all night, pacing, looking out into the street, holding the memory stick in my hand. I think about how peaceful our estate looks when everyone's asleep, how it takes on some kind of otherworldly quality, like it's not a real place, just lots of little doll's houses sitting next to each other. I think about how so many people on this street have almost become like those little dolls that can be moved around randomly, how people like Mike and Abreshima and Ali have been lifted from elsewhere and placed into somewhere they never belonged, but from the outside you'd never be able to tell the difference. Which is the point, I suppose.

'They'll be positioning them with families here, making them speak a language that isn't theirs, all in the name of doing something good,' Lloyd had said.

My Lloyd, the futurologist. Even as he was slipping away, he could envisage it all. How I'd grieve, how I'd get angry, how I'd get jealous, how I'd do the impulsive thing. He saw it all, when I couldn't even foresee what I would do the next minute, hour, day.

I hear Ali come into the house. He's been with Abreshima for hours, planning their getaway, I assume. I've seen Mike come out into the forecourt a few times and look around, as if he's looking for something, but then Melissa all too often comes to the door and calls him back in. I see the anguished look on replacement Mike's face, caught now between the future he's dipped into by coming here and getting Melissa pregnant and the past that's being flaunted in his face by Ali and Abreshima. I can see the tough choice they are making – after all, Abreshima and Ali are family, Mike isn't. Mike – though he doesn't know it or remember – chose his own destiny through his terrible actions and deeds.

The door opens and Ali comes in. I can hear him near me, breathing...

'I can still give you what you want,' he says, edging closer. 'We could try... if you want...'

I turn. I'm angry now, at Lloyd's plan. Thinking it would be as easy as that; that I'd be fine with some complete stranger turning up, offering to be a father to my baby. The future I'd envisaged – of me and him and our child

– is never going to be possible. Why would I replace it with some other reality? Why doesn't anyone accept their circumstances anymore?

'I don't want anything from you!' I say. 'I could send you back, I could be done with all this nonsense and...'

'You could,' he says, 'of course you could. And that would be your right.'

'My future is gone,' I say. It comes out more like a whisper. I'm shocked at the brutality of it. Gone. All of it, Lloyd, the baby we could have had, all of it.

'Yes, but mine isn't,' he says. 'You could give me mine back, if you wanted to.'

It occurs to me in that moment that Lloyd knew I'd be facing this choice at some point. Me, who never even noticed that Melissa's first husband had died, who hadn't spoken two words to Mrs Evermoor until she was needed, me who was happy living in my little bubble with Lloyd, never needing anyone else. Me, who thought only of me, mostly.

Suddenly I hear the sound of a siren, far off. An ambulance comes thundering down our street and comes to a halt outside Mike and Melissa's place. Two paramedics rush out and into the house. As soon as they are in, I see Abreshima come running out of her own house and stand in front of ours, looking up at the window.

As Ali turns to look at me, I know what this means. It means: there is no more time. My decision has to come now.

'I'll get my car keys,' I say.

Before we leave, I post the memory stick through Melissa's door in an envelope with a note to ask her not to look at it right now, but to keep it safe for me, for future use.

Chapter 17

It isn't until we're nearly out of town that I realise I'm still in my dressing gown and slippers. Abreshima is in the back seat with Ali, trying to remove his tag with her secateurs. I hear much commotion in a language I don't understand.

'Be careful you don't cut his foot off,' I say.

I don't want blood on the backseat; I don't want the authorities thinking I murdered Ali and Abreshima as well as everything else.

There is a sudden yelp of pain from the back seat as Ali's tag is removed by force and Abreshima hurls it out through the open window, where I hear it smash to bits on the pavement. Once a tag gets removed and deactivated, it sends out a signal to the Replacement Centre, Abreshima says, so she has made me drive at least twenty miles in the wrong direction until that happens, to make it look like they are escaping to the airport, when in fact, they are going to board a ferry in a completely different part of the country.

I do a U turn and we head into the night, in the direction of the nearest port. Abreshima says there are people working on the inside at the checkpoints too who will usher them through and give them crew member outfits. In an hour's time they will have slipped into another reality altogether. Something they are becoming used to, all part of the process of going back to being who they were, Abreshima says.

No one speaks for a whole hour on our way down there. Ali sits in the back seat with his head down and looks like he's praying. Abreshima looks out of the window, expressionless, bag on her lap. I put my foot down in my furry slippers and push onwards, deep into the night, ignoring my phone pinging next to me. Abreshima keeps picking up my phone and sighing, reporting that it's the Replacement Centre, who have come to do a spot check as a result of the birth of the baby and have found no one at home. They have left countless answerphone messages asking if I could confirm the whereabouts of my replacement. The phone rings incessantly and we listen to it, knowing that with every call the chances of this actually working are slim.

I pull into the car park and sit there quietly for a few minutes, exhausted from the long drive. Abreshima cups my face in her hand and says, 'You did something good, OK? You may not have wanted to, or planned it, but you did something good.'

With that she gets out of the car. I catch my final glimpse of Ali, looking so much like Lloyd that it hurts, giving me one final goodbye wave in the rearview mirror. It's the goodbye I never had from Lloyd, the Lloyd who was too weak to raise his hand to say goodbye to me. I nod and sit there quietly as they depart and walk into the blackness surrounding us, but not before Abreshima hands me a letter, slipping it into the front seat of the car.

It has Lloyd's handwriting on the front.

Chapter 18

The paper smells of vanilla and marzipan and is so fine it almost comes apart in my hands. I can just make out Lloyd's terrible handwriting: doctor's handwriting, we used to joke.

Forgive me the brevity of this letter, my love, it says. But if you are reading this, all I can say is that I'm very proud of you. Of us. Of what we managed to achieve, without letting death come between us. It proves you can control the future, and do good, even from your own grave.

My hands are trembling. Lloyd is talking to me again. For the first time since he died. All this time, in that house, with Ali, and Mrs Evermoor, he's been all around me and I've been so angry with him for not being there.

I can only say I love you, and am sorry to have had to leave you like I did. But my death means someone else can be free. These people deserve more than having to live our little mundane lives in our cul-de-sacs, they deserve to live the life they want, like you do. Like I did. Thank you for granting

Abreshima and Ali the chance to live again.

I can barely read the rest of the letter through my tears. I look up and see the glittering lights of the ferry in the distance. Suddenly, there is an urge in me to see this through, to go right to the water's edge and to see that boat float away, to prove to myself what a huge thing it was we achieved, me and Lloyd, on opposite sides of life. I turn back to see the scrawl of Lloyd's signature, and then, right beneath it, I spot another little detail, in tiny letters, as if wanting to remain undetected.

EAT ME, it says. NOW.

I lick the paper. It's wafer. Edible paper. Why on earth would he want me to eat it?

The answer presents itself to me soon enough. Lloyd's capacity for foresight has even extended to this moment now, where he knows full well, somehow, that cars will be arriving from all directions, to encircle me in the car park. He knows that this letter is the only evidence of any wrongdoing, and that once it is eaten, once it is gone, no trace of anything will be left behind.

The letter forms a clump in my throat as it goes down, the very last of Lloyd swallowed down. We are one, for a brief moment, and it feels good.

One, two, three cars all start arriving in haste in the carpark. In the dusk I can vaguely make out the shape of the woman from the Replacement Centre.

'In your own time,' someone say, over a loudspeaker, 'you can come out of the car.'

And all too suddenly I realise that they won't be after Ali and Abreshima. They expect them, after all, to want to leave, to try to escape, to break rules, to do bad. It's what they've always expected of them.

The one they're after now, after all, is me.

Chapter 19

Apparently in the fine print on the contract it noted that there would be consequences for anyone enabling a replacement to flee the agreed domestic setting. It didn't say what those consequences were, although I'm sure I will soon find out. The woman from the Replacement Centre is using a different tone entirely with me now as she bundles me into their car, shaking her head and telling the driver, 'This is the second one this week.'

They do not take me home. They take me to the place where this all started, to the Replacement Centre itself. I enter through a different door this time, a plain grey door at the back, which thuds and clangs behind me.

As they usher me down the corridor, past some of the rooms where there are women now waiting to be assessed by potential husbands, waiting to be taken home by desperate widowers. I think how desperately sad it all is, this insistence of theirs that every absence has to be filled. That people have to be made to fit. That a space can't simply be left alone.

I am taken into a room by another, younger woman and given a change of clothes. Colourless joggers and a T-shirt. She asks me to remove my clothes so they can assess them for evidence. When I ask evidence of what, she doesn't say. She turns her back while I get changed and then whisks the last of my ordinary life away in a clear plastic bag.

I sit here for what feels like hours, enjoying the plainness of the room. No windows, no furniture; it's a room that asks nothing of me but for me to be quiet and still. No clock on the wall, like time doesn't exist at all. As if I am not really living in a present without Lloyd but somewhere beyond it all, where he could still easily be alive. I lie on the floor and bring him back, conjuring him up in my mind. Hundreds of memories of my lovely Lloyd whoosh past behind my eyelids. His head bent awkwardly as we danced at our wedding, the feel of his torso under my arm in bed, the boom of his voice as he watched the evening bulletins and explained how most news stories were created by the media. His laugh. His touch. His many terrible jokes. All these things and more. He isn't absent, I want to tell them. He's in here!

The door finally opens and a woman enters. It's the same woman I met the first time I came here, the one who looked so worried in that carpark. The red hair. The frightening blue eyes.

'Mrs Denton, I'm sure you are aware that there are certain steps that need to be taken now, in order to rectify the situation we are in.'

I catch sight of the paper she has in front of her. There is a post-it note on the top of her sheet on which it reads 'Mrs Denton: new replacement?'

I laugh at the thought that they expect me to choose another husband so soon after what happened.

'Is something funny, Mrs Denton?' the woman asks.

'It would be,' I say, 'if it wasn't so sad. Do you honestly think choosing another replacement is what needs to happen here, after everything? Do you really still think what you're doing here is good?'

The woman looks up at me with a strange look on her face.

'I don't think you understand, Mrs Denton. Your breach of contract means that we now have the right to proceed in the way we think is the most suitable.'

'But I don't want another replacement, I just

want to go home…'

'Home is just an idea, really, isn't it?' the woman answers, never once taking her eyes off the paperwork. 'This is what we tell all our residents, when they first come here. That it's just an idea they've created in their head of where they belong. Who's to say where anyone truly belongs? Aren't we creatures who can adjust to our habitat, wherever we are? All home is really is a set of choices, a set of circumstances.'

It's like there's a train headed right for me, and I can see it travelling at speed down a tunnel as she speaks.

'I want to go…' I am surprised by how weak my own voice sounds in this room, like all the power's been drained from it.

'Home, yes, you said. But I'm afraid if you're referring to the property where you currently reside then that's been handed over to us, for the time being, as was the contractual obligation in these circumstances….'

'What, no, that can't be…'

'So now we need to move on to the matter of relocating a replacement…'

'I don't want a replacement!' I try to scream, but nothing comes out but a pathetic whimper.

'Oh, we won't be getting you a replacement,

Mrs Denton, don't you worry about that.'

She looks up at me and smiles.

'This time, you *are* the replacement.'

Chapter 20

It doesn't take me all that long to settle in. Perhaps the woman from the Centre was right, maybe home is just a strange idea, and that there isn't that much difference between sitting in my sparkling clean kitchen in my new-build house and sitting in a tiny box room with a TV and only one window.

In a strange way I feel closer to Lloyd here than I did in my old home. After all, I'm inside the institution he was fascinated by for so long, the place he was trying to understand, the place he was trying to change. Everyone knows you can't change anything from the outside. You need to be on the inside to make a real difference.

I am now surrounded by women who have experienced a loss exactly like my own. When I say exactly, I've come to understand that no one's loss is the same, no single absence is felt with quite the same intensity. Some women here never even had time to prepare for the worst, their husbands simply expired in a flash of smoke or disappeared suddenly. I have learnt to be grateful for the time I had with Lloyd, knowing what was coming, however awful that was. That I got to bury him and that I got to understand him better through Ali and Abreshima, these are tiny little joys that I now take comfort in, because there was a side to Lloyd I never would have seen unless he'd died and a path I would never have chosen if it wasn't for him leaving it in the first place.

At night, when the wardens let us talk, these women and I share stories of our husbands, our lovers, the children we had or the children we hoped to have, and keep them alive, for ourselves and for each other. When we pass each other on the corridors we don't just see each other, we see our absences too. We imagine them as presences, walking next to us. Many of the women greet me and Lloyd on the corridor, as if he's just a few steps behind me, trying to catch up.

Which, in many ways, I think he is. For all his foresight, he must never have anticipated this kind of future. One in which I fill that space not with another husband, or a child, but with the kindness and friendship of these women. With their voices, their stories.

But we have to be careful. The wardens of the Replacement Centre watch us closely. Sometimes we have to rein it in, pretend not to be friends, to ignore each other, so that they won't be able to work out what it is we're up to.

Because we have a plan, these women and I, a plan to make the most of our positions, when we are chosen as replacements.

A plan Lloyd put in place without knowing it. Because what happened when I replaced him with Ali was that I never replaced him at all. I was the one who was replaced. The old me. The me who never noticed those around me – what they were doing, what they were suffering, who they had lost.

When we go out into those homes our aim is to change the people who take us on. To make them see those absences at the heart of themselves.

Once that is replaced, the future is ours.